Let Me Taste

A Creative Novella

Kendra M. Harris, PhD

Published by Nine Pages Media
asiarainey@gmail.com
www.ninepagesmedia.com

Cover concept and design by Shaddai Livingston.
Cover final design/formatting by Nine Pages Media [9PM].

This book is dedicated to my mother, Linda Marie Harris Copprue, her parents, Walter and Georgiana Harris, and their eldest daughter, Shirley M. Harris. It is also dedicated to my father, Charles "Fluker" Hudson and his parents, Luther Hudson and Lizzie Mae Forman. ...and to my dearest sister-friend, Shelley Patrice Baham.

I vow to carry every ounce of wisdom, foundation, and tools for perseverance of which they have instilled in me. ...until I take my last breath.

Say their names
Iba'se

~

Contents

Introduction

Let Me Taste is Karasi's creative story, from the book *Laced Bloodline* (2011), written as she faced twists on her journey to safety from Hurricane Katrina. She often retreated to a place in her mind that silenced turmoil on that journey. Poetry, figurative writing, creative monologues, and her dreams were doodled in a journal. *Let Me Taste* is that story.

Karasi tells a story about family, endurance, love, and healing. She paints a beautiful ole school 90's hip-hop love story. However, her main character stands parentless at seventeen and into her young adult years under the protection of her aunt. There is pain from loss. There is hopeless love. There is grief. There is laughter and beauty. There is life.

What happens when transitions, pain, and grief are not addressed? Do we only continue to move forward? Does that work? Can it be addressed with laughter and love, acceptance and music used as vehicles to move forward by common beliefs and behaviors? This is a short story that shows the ever so repeated cycle of love, loss, pain, and joy in New Orleans.

Remember to stick around through the pages of this book for the author's commentary. The commentary briefly explains the resilience of a politically oppressed group of people situated densely in one geographical space.

Harris points to thriving underlined generational beliefs and behaviors subsisting with shared culture, which is lived experience whether researched with logic or with empirical lens. Shared culture, passed through generations, is life for constructively defined black communities in New Orleans.

Faultless Yellow

Tiye

Karasi: Note to self –
Remember to finish the story in my journal

Potential title: Let Me Taste

Emotional colors masking dissipating despair
Every human sense, in this moment, alert but unprepared for
honeysuckle scented inhales pumping soft iridescent
message hues
to the brain stem. Silent screams wail, shooting hard-shocked
visual indigo blues
but I'm with him
And I'm open
Hoping he catch the rhythms of each sporadic wave down my
back.
Wanting him to squeeze the largest curve of me and breathe
at the nape of my neck.
I'm open
Soaking up all my walls more with each nibble
Tremble at every thigh tingle as we toss and turn
Unconsciously parting my lips more with each playful bite and
caress,
wondering which other parts will he address and learn
Melting
Sparked coal
Moistened onyx skin
Rub placing and tasting buds
Out and in
Loving how our souls are being nourished and felt
Our limbs wrapped around each other like an octopus belt.
I'm open
Licking and sucking and pulling and kiss

4

Breathing and swelling and pinching and this…
the entry and my bliss
And his groans and my moans and my muscles and my skin
and our tussles
And our toes and his chill bumps and my sweat, on his neck
My cheek smashed against the delicate hairs on his chest
And stubble on his cheeks and his neck, sensational rest
And my breast on his tongue
Nipples erect.
And our fingers, at their tips, down our cracks react like fate.
Then, the hairs on our bodies stood straight.
I'm open
Sweet melodic baritone in my ear
Closed lids sight ocean waves under sunset while dropping
tears.
The relief. No fear.
The release. No words
but at least, no grief.
We smiled.

The Calinda is the dance I danced in my dream. It is the dance of the ancestors when they celebrated self and invited one another into relationships. I was always adorned with soft, flowing white linen that dragged behind as I stepped forward with a tall beautiful head wrap that shimmered. The air released a romantic scent that hypnotized us as we inhaled and you took my hand, in my dream.

~

Summer days in New Orleans are filled with festivals and outdoor concerts. It's when I love New Orleans the most. In every love affair, the good has to be taken with the bad. And man, the heat and rain in July is bad.

But I love it, nevertheless. We were splashing through the grass watered by nature in Marconi Meadows to get to the stage because Doug E. Fresh was up next. As it began to rain, the crowd scattered and we moved up closer. They all came out at once to see what was going on with the showers. Po' Righteous Teachers, Rob Base, Pharcyde, A Tribe Called Quest, Doug E. Fresh, Slick Rick, MC Lyte, Big Daddy Kane; all I needed was Eric B. and Salt n' Pepper. Then, I would have felt as if I traveled back through time. I was high. I floated on the sound waves and rode with the hip hop caravan to old school bliss. Those were my days. Those days held my bold vivaciousness. Those days held my "get out my way" attitude. In those days, I would have never let the love of my life keep on passing me by. Doug E. Fresh started beat boxing so the others gave him room. They exited the stage.

Hello, lady. How are you? It was one of the men getting into an elevator as I headed home from my research class. They perspired as if they had just finished working out. They wore sweats and carried odd shaped duffle bags. The man who said hello wore a smile that shouted many more greetings than the "how are you" greeting heard.

He wore smooth dark skin and a crown of free nearly natty hair. From that moment he watched me dance. From a distance, I danced and sang crescendo tones for the one who greeted me. I included him in every decision made, but only if he knew. Or did he? His eyes carried the deepest glance that housed non-tangible intimacy. His stare burned the protective layer of skin that hid the sparkling shade of love that glistened all over me.

"He knew," I often thought to myself. He knew! We became friends. I introduced him to my family. We shared family. We shared stories from back in the day when hip hop was our life. We shared stories expressing what truly was the making of the person standing before me or the making of the person standing before him. We shared recipes, instruments, ideas, and concerns. I shared my heart. And he knew! Did he?

We held hands and twirled around on sacred ground as we both inhaled the hypnotic aroma. The sweetest scent nestled the air arousing our wilds as we moved from holding hands to a full embrace. I saw Oshun as she moved her mirror toward me to shine my reflection within view. She then gave me a bouquet to remind me that I am just as charming. We swayed without a smile. I fell in love with you, in my dream.

I'm surrounded by white smoke such as clouds
And I see, ahead of me, a man, standing in a bright gleam
With open arms reaching out to me, proudly
And I, hoping to be drawn closer and closer to him
But...suddenly the lights are beginning to appear dim
But still he's reaching and waiting,
Patiently waiting with a flow'r-
In his mouth, the stem
Finally, we've met, and petals fall
and the wind gently begins to blow

In the parking lot of my apartment complex in Treme, where we all hung out, was the place I stood when I fell in love with hip hop. I remember looking over through the fence to see what was going on under the Claiborne Bridge. I remember smiling at the "Dope is Death" banner that blew in the wind as the cars sped on I-10 east. I saw the usual folks playing their boom boxes as they did a syncopated skip to the brass band melodies blasting from the speakers. There were always people under the bridge.

Even as I fell asleep, their voices blared through my window. I heard cars pass with the stereos playing a song my mama loved so much. She had the album. I can still see it. The cover was sky blue. The color I see now when I think of hip hop. Rapper's Delight had a sound that was unique to me. I listened to music by Odis Redding and Aretha Franklin; I guess you could say I've always had an old soul. I was influenced by the songs sung by Etta James and Billie Holiday.

I fantasized about being there to place my eyes on Nina Simone when she sang of Mississippi. Goddamn, I must have been there! But now, I listened to a man say, "hip – hop - ahibby- ahibby ahibby;" he was rocking! What I heard was not a test! He was rocking to the beat. I began to clothe myself with those words and I wanted to know more. Where did he come from? What is this music? I had heard nothing that carried the sort of beat that transformed the very beat of my heart. But from that point on, my heart played hip hop beats pumping out poetic lyrics to flow through my veins.

My friends and I started bringing our boom boxes outside to listen to this hip hop as we played baseball with sticks from broken window seals and shell rocks that posed as pavement in the parking lot. When a car window was hit, we all would break out running down the street but never leaving the music behind. We ran down Governor Nicholls St. to see some crazy boys spin on their head. It was a new dance. All lined up around a piece of linoleum lying on the ground, they clapped and jumped from side to side before they, unbelievably, spun at record speed on their backs, their shoulders, their knees, and their heads. It was incredible! And they played the same music, hip hop. What did they know that I didn't know?

They were older. Maybe they had been to New York. New York was the place I found the music to come. Boogie Down Productions represented South Bronx. Heavy D represented "money earning Mount Vernon." I wanted to go there, but since I was still in elementary school it was unlikely.

As the days passed, I carried a weight inside of me that was too heavy to ignore. I had to make a quest and since I was too young to leave New Orleans alone, I had to make my own New York - where hip hop lived. Things were changing though. My mama, now, wanted me to catch the bus to my new school. She said with her going to work, she had no time to bring me to school. She said I was getting older and it was time for me to learn to get around the city.

My mama worked as hard as anybody trying to make the ends meet. She couldn't keep a schedule that included transportation for me. So, I learned to catch the public bus. The Sunday evening before I entered the seventh grade, she walked me to the bus stop and we waited for the St. Bernard bus to come. We boarded the bus and rode all of the way to my new school and home again.

We didn't walk back home though. She walked home to get her car and followed the bus as she made me get back on the next bus to arrive. By myself. My mama drove behind the bus and took me home when I got off at the right stop. On the bus, all I could think of was how relieved I was that she never knew I was responsible for her cracked windshield. I never told her. It was just an itsy-bitsy crack anyway. It was a lesson learned, both the bus and the crack.

From then on, I learned by doing. Making mistakes most of the time but *doing*, nonetheless. I became strong and independent as a junior high school student. On the bus, I learned all there was to know about hip hop. I learned names, and beats, and life stories of the artists.

I learned, first-hand, what the music I so adored was really expressing – survival. The music helped me to sharpen my memory. I began to remember clearly and understand the times in my young life when I felt pain. The music gave the mental place I lived a name, *the jungle*, and I was close to the edge. Hip Hop became my friend and we shared everything. I continued writing poetry to release that pain, like my friend advised. We were inseparable.

To me, I was hip hop. I wore Salt n' Pepper earrings and had the flyest stacks in the city, even a stacked gheri curl. My jeans were artistically carved and my shoes were Adidas. If I had a problem, my friend was there always to comfort me. Hip hop always knew what to say.

Summer days in New Orleans are filled with festivals and outdoor concerts. It's when I love New Orleans the most. In every love affair, the good has to be taken with the bad. And, man, the heat and rain in July is bad. But I love it, nevertheless. We were splashing through the grass watered by nature in Marconi Meadows to get to the stage because Doug E. Fresh was up next. As it began to rain again, the crowd scattered and we moved up closer. Kolunde and I was consoled and comforted by the rhythm of the rain drops. Po' Righteous Teachers, Rob Base, Pharcyde, A Tribe Called Quest, Doug E. Fresh, Slick Rick, Big Daddy Kane; all I needed was Eric B. and Salt n' Pepper. Then, I would have felt as if I traveled back through time. I was high. I floated on the sound waves and rode with the hip hop caravan to old school bliss. We looked up, opened our arms wide and stuck out our tongues.

Spiced Brown

Tiye

~

As I sat in the class with worry of the content held by the upcoming mid-term exam, I listened to a peculiar sound that traveled from quite a distance in the building. Although slightly muffled, it was too clear to be someone's radio. I found relaxation in that rhythmic sound. It was drumming.

I was able to hear every naked palm slap the drum, making a honey-hollow noise and able to hear the quick tongued fingertips as they counter created a melody for an African journey. Soon, I was fully submerged in this melody, forgetting the anxiety carried as my professor lectured. I was no longer in my physical, for I had embarked upon a crowded journey of serenity. The other students started to move to their perspective places when the class was over. Their movement had taken me away from my meditative state and anxiety had taken over once again.

I fastened my pace as I gathered my notebook and pen, textbook and book bag, to run to the elevators in hopes of finding the music that captivated my mind from hostility and brought an overlapping feeling of tranquility. Finally, waiting for what seemed to have been a lifetime, the doors opened. "Hello lady. How are you?" It was one of the men getting off of the elevator as I, after changing my mind about boarding the elevator, headed toward the parking lot to my car, pretending I was walking pass the elevators.

They perspired as if they had just finished working out. They wore sweats and carried odd shaped duffle bags. The man who said hello wore a smile that shouted many more greetings than the "how are you" greeting heard. He wore smooth dark skin and a crown of free nearly natted hair. Oh, I thought to myself, he is beautiful! Overwhelmed, I ran toward my car. Mentally. It seemed as if my feet just didn't move swiftly enough to get me out of such an awkward spot.

This man began to walk with me. "Hello," he said again, wearing the brightest smile I had ever seen on a man's face. "Hi," I replied, looking at my Adidas. We began to exchange words that were small in spoken word but huge in spirit, soon becoming best friends in a word. He walked me to my car taking the keys from my hand. New Orleans men are just that bold. Mystery leaned over to unlock the door. Displaying a character that smelled of truth, he opened the door wishing me a warm goodnight and welcoming a tomorrow's hello.

During my drive home, I continued to smell that fragrance he wore. It was musky and sweaty but a sensual scent no one could probably pull off but him. I wondered about his life. Was he a drummer only for the class that took in two floors above the one I was on? Or, was he a professional drummer who carried with him this scent on his African journey of serenity? Was he the King for whom I awaited? What would he be going home to face tonight? I felt as if I was a silly schoolgirl handing over a note that read:

DO YOU LIKE ME?

YES   NO   MAYBE

Or sending my mystery love schoolgirl poetry such as:

> When I first met you, I knew you were a flirt
> Although I fell in love with you, I knew I would get hurt
> I tried to tie you down to me, only one
> Trying to do something no one's ever done
> Now you want our love to end and I try not to cry
> Trying so very hard to learn to kiss your lips good-bye
> With my sorrow and tears, I'll always be there
> Trying to find a love, one I don't have to share

I had begun to finish this love affair before it even started. I guess that is what I had been accustomed to in my life. I had never experienced sweet tastes on my tongue. There were never good things for me.

His eyes carried the deepest glance that housed non-tangible intimacy. His stare burned the protective layer of skin that hid the sparkling shade of love that glistened all over me. "He knew," I often thought to myself. He knew! We shared stories from back in the day when hip hop was our life. We shared stories expressing what truly was the making of the person standing before me or the making of the person standing before him. We shared recipes, instruments, ideas, and concerns. I shared my heart. And he knew!

I believe he knew of all the guarded love I detained. It was amazing how I expected this man to know what was inside of me. After all, he was just learning me. I was learning him, but absorbed more of his soul with each communicable moment.

I wanted him to know my wounds. I wanted him to know my insecurities. I wanted him to know my heart; the cut-out in my heart had been measured and tailored for him. He is in my dreams.

"No, I'm not doing that again." "I'm done with trying to have a happily ever after love story. It doesn't work for me," Tiye said as she sat throwing lumps of hardened dirt onto the pavement watching it crack with every impact. "I won't be telling the story of my change in relationships – how some mother neglected to embrace her son and now he's grown with overly affectionate issues or how society has pounced on some brother and left a docile man as a shell of anger waiting to explode soon unable to utilize his own judgment." "It's not like that!" he said.

"In your life, make sure the man you chose has passion for something in his life other than you, and then he will know how to love you," said Kolunde as he held Tiye's grimy hand, tilting his head around the edge of her face to make eye contact. "You have to be wise enough to see his soul, Tiye." "Anyway, you going to Michigan next week? I was hoping you could stop by my cousin's house to check on him. They say he's not doing well but I need to see him; I'll send your eyes. It's been about a year and a half since we saw him." It had only been about a year and a half since Kolunde met him, but they became instant brothers.

Tiye changed the subject of conversation to avoid looking into Kolunde's deep brown stare that told a story from the ancestors with each momentary look. She stood and brushed the grass from her ankle length dress which covered her naked body as she waited for his answer.

"Yes, I am going. Give me his address. I need to talk to my brother anyway." "I haven't seen him since he moved up there. Cancer, huh?! Yeah, we need to rap on some spiritual healing – he'll be alright!" Tiye hugged Kolunde as she said goodnight. "It's 2:00 in the morning" she realized as they sat underneath an oak tree in City Park near the carousal. "I guess I'll go home and get some sleep. You get some sleep too and I'll talk to you tomorrow."

As Kolunde held Tiye to send with her well wishes for the night, she allowed her body to be seen with a touch when he closed his eyes. She shared her soft caresses that were saved for him but rationed for their lengthy goodnight or morning hugs. It was those times when they held the most intimate conversations. It was those times when he would tell her how much he yearned for a woman who was an extension of him, but one who was a nurturer, a caregiver.

With his eyes closed, he told her she was beautiful when he leaned toward her carefully, never to physically touch her but close enough for them to smell the fragrance of lust in the air they were breathing. Tiye was paralyzed at these times. She longed for him to remove the elusive fence that held her on the friendship block of their build-a-relationship game board. But he just kept her there, at friendship, gazing at her and hugging her.

Kolunde was a concert promoter. He traveled often to view potential venues for shows. Although he booked the biggest names in hip hop, he scouted venues that were in areas known to be violent and impoverished. This is where hip hop progressed, and this is where hip hop is appreciated the most because it is where the lyrics are born.

This is where people knew what it was to be hungry, to survive the struggle. He dealt with many artists, but they had to be special kinds of artists who had not been changed into a "larger than the Creator" life form. They had to be people who live their lyrics and send positive messages through their songs.

In Tiye's eyes, Kolunde was a decent brotha. He was sensitive but strong, mellow but mighty, and passionate about his people. She went to the concerts that were no more than three hours away. True, it was because she loved the music but also because she felt Kolunde's presence in her soul whenever she was next to anything he touched.

We shared stories from back in the day when hip hop was our life. We shared stories expressing what truly was the making of the person standing before me or the making of the person standing before him. I introduced him to my family. We shared family. We shared recipes, percussion instruments, ideas and concerns. I shared my heartbeat. And he knew! I believe he knew of all the guarded love I detained. It was amazing how I expected this man to know what was inside of me.

After all, he was just learning me. I was learning him but absorbed more of his soul with each communicable moment. There was a sad place in his soul that I wanted to explore. I wanted him to know my wounds. I wanted him to know my insecurities. I wanted him to know my heart; the cut out had been measured and tailored for him. He is in my dreams.

As we swayed, standing on clouds and listening to the African sounds of Alpha Blondy delicately roving through the atmosphere, we smiled. We walked, together, on the edges of paradise, hand in hand, without a word uttered but a soothing vibe that told a million stories. With your eyes, you told me that I am your wife, as you rubbed your hand along the nape of my neck. And I, quivering inside as I slightly rolled my neck leaning toward what felt so good.

My hair became exposed and it began to cover my face, but you brushed it away and stared. Still without a word, you moved your hand through my natural tresses with one hand and gently grasped my hips with the other. I slowly moved to the chimes of the melody playing, symbolically tasting the sweet. There we stood on the edge of paradise, wanting, in my dream.

Indigo Blue

Kolunde

~

On the corner of St. Claude Ave. and Alabo in the CTC, ['cross the canal,' New Orleans' lower ninth ward], my cousin and I would stand choosing cars as they zoomed by to have as our own. I always chose the older modeled cars. My mama say I was an old soul since birth. The ancestors have walked with me ever since. We played marbles in the dirt next to the tracks, but as little dudes we often had real big men ideas. I told my cousin I was going to spread positive energy throughout the world through some kind of art form. I just wasn't sure which art form. I told him that I smell death and our people are killing themselves. We listened to Triggerman on a cassette tape playing in our boom box. As we bobbed our heads and plucked marbles, we made a pact to always spread the good word.

I watched my sister submit to the ways of a two-cent prostitute so she could get high. She started robbing people, killing people, and blowing her punk ass two-bit pimp when he was tired of her vagina that had only been innocent for the first year of her life. She came home pregnant! My mama hadn't seen her for four months. But "she popped up pregnant," my mama said. I had seen her. I used to follow her when she went on her escapades. Tamalah never knew though.

I was eleven years old; she was fourteen, and I wanted to know why she wasn't at home. I watched her make her money. I watched her buy heroin or crack somebody in the head for their wallet but then get strong armed and raped. I went to take up for her. She was so high she never knew I was there. I wanted to protect her but her "friends" would just push me to the ground and call my sister all kind of messed up names. They told me that I would be just like her. An addict.

I ran whenever I saw a gun, ran all the way home to my daddy to tell him what I had seen Tamalah do. He told me, very calmly and matter-of-factly, "Your sister is dead." But Daddy...all it took was for him to raise his hand and I was silenced. I remember when he told me he would kill me if I told him anything else about my sister. I believed him. My sister has hurt him so much that in his mind he rather know her as dead than a living mistake of his, tarnished with the family's secret. He blamed himself for my sister's addiction.

"Why my baby!" I heard him cry out to seemingly no one, one night as I peeked through the curtain that separated the hall from the living room where I slept. He was on his knees and then his stomach, stretched out flat, wailing and vomiting because he was drunk. "I trusted that bastard to babysit," my daddy blurted often but I never knew what he was talking about. Due to a computer error that let him out early, my father had just come home from Angola for shooting his brother to death for raping his daughter. Tamalah was two and my cousin, Sage, was born that year.

He was born one year before me, but he carried such wisdom that made him seem a whole lot older. When his daddy died, his mama killed herself after giving birth, so my mama took him as her own. Sage would tell me about him and Tamalah growing up. He said he hated her because she was the reason his father was gone. And that he hated my daddy because he killed his daddy. I just shook my head and folded my arms because I knew this dude wasn't gon' sit here on these tracks and tell me that he hated my mama too! If it wasn't for her, he would surely be missing. But he said he loved my mama and that it was confusing to him how she could love him so after what happened.

He said my mother told him, "This is what's going to happen, African child. You will be a respectful and well-respected man. You will have a heart filled with love and I will love you forever, my son." He said Tamalah was a jewel to my mama, but she was eccentric to him. She was nervous all of the time. She shook with tremors involuntarily. Po' thing! Sage told me what he overheard the grown-ups in the neighborhood talking about.

My mama found Tamalah one day in the closet in my uncle's room bleeding from her mouth and her private parts. Uncle Sage was high and had forgotten her there. They said that it had happened before, but my uncle would clean her up and put her to bed before my parents came home from work.

The men on the corner, who stood there with beers in their hand in front of the store, explained to each other what my uncle had told them. They said my uncle said that he would get rock-hard whenever he picked her up because her flower was "so fresh and innocent." They would tell each other how he pushed his rock-hard dick inside of her, pushing and pushing, and pushing until her little body was forced opened to accept him. They talked about how my uncle would say he jabbed his dick to the back of her throat until she threw up and made her suck, then did her anally.

Nobody knew what to do for her, but for the rest of her life my mother held and squeezed her, never wanting to let her go. I guess my mother was grieving because in her mind she had lost her little girl to her brother-in-law. She watched her child die emotionally. But Tamalah was two! I never understood how she relived all of this – she was only two years old. But my mother relived it for the rest of her life, grieving herself to death. There was no escaping.

My sister came home. And there was time, after all, to bond with her. My hopes were subsided when I learned Tamalah was only home to steal some things from the house. After I hugged her, smelling her inborn perfume scent of leaves from a magnolia tree topped with the sweet mellifluous aroma of amber, I gave her my Atari and my school clothes. But it wasn't enough for her. She must have been in trouble with someone.

Tamalah was shot and killed that night. She died two nights before my mother transitioned of "natural causes," the doctors said. But she died from grief and a broken heart, I say. Tamalah killed my mama. Two nights prior, she was caught climbing out of a window of a brightly multi-colored house on Caffin Avenue with a jewelry box. The bullet went into her left shoulder blade and came out of the right side of her neck.

Yeah, daddy, my sister is dead. And my mama too!

We sat staring - me, my daddy and lil Sage, listening to Triggerman in the cassette player. Soon, they had no love for what was truly beautiful. My daddy and Sage were left docile men. They became shells of anger waiting to explode soon unable to utilize their own judgment. And hip hop became my parent, serving as a bullhorn which echoed the voices of the ancestors.

Lash to back
They roped his neck
They whipped, beat, gore, blood, was castrated
They starve, scorn, was dehumanized
They suffered for my dignity
I am King with pride given by them
I am child of Congo Square
I am Africans tainted by the New World
I am wounded, though never was I there
But the hurt is when I can just remember

Tiye revisited her dream:

We shared stories from back in the day when hip hop was our life. We shared stories expressing what truly was the making of the person standing before me or the making of the person standing before him. We shared recipes, instruments, ideas and concerns. I shared my heart. And he knew! I believe he knew of all the guarded love I detained. It was amazing how I expected this man to know what was inside of me. After all, he was just learning me. I was learning him but absorbed more of his soul with each communicable moment. There was a sad place in his soul that I wanted to explore. I wanted him to know my wounds. I wanted him to know my insecurities. I wanted him to know my heart; the cut out had been measured and tailored for him. He is in my dreams.

Standing in the rain, we were as happy as school-aged students at Christmas time. We were just standing there, free with no school. Freshmen year was in the books. We were rocking to the best concert ever to hit the streets of New Orleans for this summer of festivals. Doug E. Fresh blew up the spot when Slick Rick stepped onto the stage. La-Di-Da-Di is a classic! Kolunde took my hand and we left backstage to go into the audience front and center, like we both did in the old days. In that moment, we had forgotten all of our worries. We were smiling, dancing and rapping as if we were on stage while everyone stood and looked from their respective shelters, hiding from the rain.

Striking Orange

In The Gambia, with a Brooklyn State of Mind

After Tiye graduated from Starks University in New Orleans, she became a Professor at The University of Gambia in Banjul. She loved The Gambia. Life for her was fully defined in West Africa. Many streets, to her, resembled what she had missed from her home in New Orleans. She would often stand at the tip top balcony of a twenty-five-foot, hand built Islamic tower that stood over the city. Tiye remembered watching men dressed in old t-shirts and shorts with nothing but leather sandals, also hand-made, to protect their feet. She watched them make cinder blocks from mud and place them one brick at a time to build unbelievably sturdy buildings. She watched them make the building's infrastructure of iron, rebar and steel mesh, and wrought-iron railings for those building with cordless irons used to unwrinkle clothing that held only burning charcoal for heat. She watched, from that tower, as people walked along the streets of Banjul, the streets that looked like Decatur Street in New Orleans.

Nevertheless, she would often wonder and even long for her friend Kolunde. Kolunde now lived in Brooklyn, New York and had given up on concert promotion because he said hip hop was dead. He was found in deep thought two and three times in a day because, to himself, he would whisper "Hip Hop's not really dead. It's just real cats aren't heard anymore!" "Everybody wanna be a gangsta."

His heart couldn't let go of what had kept him sane in his life. "I wanna savor the eclectic threads that were woven to make me who I am, and those threads are the phrases from rhythmic words combined with def melodies that grip hip hop culture."

Ultimately, Kolunde was homesick. Being away always feels like exile for anyone born in New Orleans. New Orleans is a country within a country. It has its own society of culture bearers who step outside of life as the rest of the country knew it to take a deep breath and live. Although people worked for a living just as everyone else, which is not believed by the rest of the U.S., they appreciated what was most important. People in New Orleans worked to live, not the other way around.

Kolunde, with the soul of an artist, missed his country. He ended up living in Brooklyn purely by accident. He was called one day by a West African dance troupe wanting to replace a drummer that had moved back home to Guinea. It was a paying gig for events surrounding the annual West Indies parade, so he decided to go until the company hired another drummer. What he didn't know was he would be the permanent drummer for all gigs. Although he didn't mind the work, he wished it had allowed him to remain in New Orleans. But unfortunately for him all of the shows, for the past three years, were in the north, on the northeast coast. As Kolunde played Sorsoner, a traditional West African rhythm, for a show in Newark, he thought of the dream Tiye had. He remembered her raspy voice and heavily New Orleanian accented dialect…

"The Calinda is the dance I danced in my dream. It is the dance of the ancestors when they celebrated self and invited one another into relationships. I was always adorned with soft, flowing white linen that dragged behind as I stepped forward with a tall beautiful head wrap that shimmered. The air released a romantic scent that hypnotized us as we inhaled and you took my hand, in my dream. We held hands and twirled around on sacred ground as we both inhaled the hypnotic aroma. The sweetest scent nestled the air arousing our wilds as we moved from holding hands to a full embrace. I saw Oshun; she handed me honey, as she moved her mirror toward me to shine my reflection within view. She then gave me a bouquet to remind me that I am just as charming.

We swayed without a smile. I fell in love with you, in my dream. As we swayed, standing on clouds and listening to the African sounds of Alpha Blondy delicately roving through the atmosphere, we smiled. We walked, together, on the edges of paradise, hand in hand, without a word uttered but a soothing vibe that told a million stories. With your eyes, you told me that I am your wife, as you rubbed your hand along the nape of my neck. And I, quivering inside as I slightly rolled my neck leaning toward what felt so damn good. My hair became exposed and it began to cover my face but you brushed it away and stared. Still without a word, you moved your hand though my natural tresses with one hand and gently grasped my hips with the other. I slowly moved to the chimes of the melody playing."

There we stood on the edge of paradise, wanting, in my dream.

Kolunde realized that he had really missed Tiye just as much as he missed New Orleans. Even more. But, for years, he never admitted that he knew of her truly unconditional deep romantic love for him. He kept her believing that he only saw her as a childhood friend, as close as true bonds kept a brothers and sisters. He knew she was in love with him and he let her go. "I wonder if she knew?" Kolunde had been falling in love with Tiye since the first day he laid eyes on her at Starks U. He thought she had a strange vibe about her that intrigued him, subdued him.

Playing the second half of the show, he remembered when the elevator doors opened and placing his eyes on Tiye as she stood there waiting for him and his friends to get out off of the elevator. He remembered that Tiye acted like she was walking by the elevator and not waiting to go up. He wondered if she was coming to meet the drumbeat. He thought, "but she was too late." Kolunde remembered how startled she looked when the doors opened and how she quickly began walking outside. It was something about her that he, being the curious cat that he was, needed to find. It was her eyes!

At the elevator, he remembered Tiye held her head down avoiding the glances from the other drummers and the piercing stare from him. It was in her eyes! Her eyes told a story that coincided with his hollowed heart. They told a familiar story tucked underneath a creative backdrop. Her eyes told her life's story. And Kolunde was drawn to her by them.

Mama Enike' was a voluptuously beautiful woman with skin that shined like wet onyx displaying her highlighted differences but paralleled color tones and exquisite bone structure. She had thick, long mahogany coarse hair that had "never been treated by the chemicals." That's what Kolunde's father would say anyway. Tiye reminded Kolunde of his mother. She looked like a younger version of Mama Enike'. Strikingly, Tiye looked just like Tamalah, Kolunde's sister. Tiye had never laid eyes on Tamalah but somehow, she moved and smelled like the two women Kolunde loved more than anything in his life, including hip hop!

Enike's youngest child had vowed to never end up like Big Alyji. He promised the great ruler of his head that he would never become an angry maimed creature who could never see past the pain in which he harbored. Kolunde held tight to his elekes. He wore those sacred beads around his neck to protect and guarantee that he would live and keep the promise he had made to himself. The necklaces, one made of six red beads patterned with six white beads and the other with seven alternating white and blue beads, was indeed the protection that guaranteed his safety according to his faith. Ifa had become the ground in which Tiye and Kolunde stood firmly upon since their teen years.

Kolunde would often fly down from New York to visit Big Alyji in New Orleans, if not for anything else but to make sure he was eating properly. He would always stop to pick up fruit to bring with him like papayas, watermelon and routinely, a blue and white plate filled with fried plantains. He would also visit the places he and Tiye frequented.

The Claiborne Bridge, to him, lost all of its exuberance now that the "Dope is Death" banner was gone. But after noticing the old guy, who had seemed to be an old man all of Kolunde's life, was still seated under the bridge with his boom box covered with a handmade tin can shield securing what was his livelihood, blasting oldies but goodies, usually Ernie K. Doe, from the speakers he remembered his daddy having when he was two years old. He felt the warmth of being home.

Kolunde would walk under the oak trees that aligned Esplanade Avenue to City Park and sit near the carousal. He remembered blissfully floating upward then downward on the black horse that Tiye loved so much. He reminisced about the day when Tiye tumbled backward in the playground area, when it was quite difficult to distinguish the grown-ups from the children playing on the swings with a quick chuckle to his self.

"I rather reminisce over you, my God," he mumbled as he headed back to his car on foot down Esplanade Avenue.

Iridescent Purple

Family Far and Near

~

My family was at their wit's end the year my cousin died. We all traveled to Michigan to comfort and console his mother. Kolunde came with us which was not surprising because he was a part of the Mercadal family ever since my parents' death. Hard times, dark trials, haunting memories – but Kolunde knew just what to say after the car accident that took my parent's life.

As he held me and rocked me that day, he explained his interpretation of the karmic cycle that took my parents - together- on that day when a pack of wild horses couldn't force them together on any other day. My parents, who disagreed on parenting, love, life, food, accidents which led to verbal fist fights in mobility packing tumultuous blows, died in a car accident. Together. On that day. They certainly couldn't find a way to live together, but they died together – on that day. The day I turned eighteen.

Kolunde loved my cousin just as much as I did. I told him that Jacques was diagnosed with cancer the day I found out. It would have certainly been beneficial to be a fly on the wall the day Kolunde visited Jacques. Whatever Kolunde said to Jacques, Aunt Rose said, "Jacques was without worry after Kolunde left." She said his face was illuminated with life, as if he had just recognized it still filled his lungs with every breath he was able to take. He was as calm as the breeze, no longer frightened of his illness. I'm not surprised though. My Kolunde was an emotional healer to all people.

As I sat on Kairaba Avenue at The Café, a restaurant in the city of Serekunda, Gambia, twenty minutes away from work in Banjul with my new family, I would drift away. Ade, my husband, always said "a penny for your thoughts." He was a kind man, very educated and well raised by his mother. I would always drift back to the life I led in the States and mentally compare the wounded brothers there to the ancestral loving men here in The Gambia. And my God, were they beautiful!

To me, they all belonged in a museum as sculptured pieces of art. Gees! I had only known men in The United States as wounded or angry, although I know better. It was my judgment that always led me to the wrong man. I felt Kolunde's hand in mine and heard his baritone voice in my head as a murmur: "make sure you choose a man who is passionate about more than only you in his life. It is then when he will know to love you."

Ade was a teacher. He taught at Ndows Comprehensive School, the family's home school in Fajara, a suburb in Serekunda. It was amazing to watch him work with the students – young boys, American dressed along with their counterparts in West African traditional attire. They were receptive to every African diasporic integrated studies lesson Mr. Campell set before them. They loved him and I did too – for what he provided me.

> *Tall, deep chocolate brown skinned,*
> *large, muscular build, nearly natty, wise, gentle man*
> *I fell I love with him*
> *He is my love*
> *Never made music*
> *I didn't want to until one year,*

Sweaty passion
Sticky love muscles
Soft tongue caresses sang crescendo tones
After time, winds had blown
and I wondered what did I do
I really did love him.
I praised his majestry.
I longed for the wisdom words that dripped from his tongue
as we mentally sat on the shores of Niger River Delta and
listened to the ancestors sing.
My skin dampened at his every diminutive touch
but the time held too much when his secret was revealed
Time held too much when I, too, had the same new secret
Two men
I loved them both for different reasons
and if combining them was an option,
I would have the perfect husband but what about him
Will his wife understand this elongated relationship on the
outer surface of matrimony? That lady's husband forever
linger around my spirit, in the spirit
That lady's husband
Tall, deep chocolate brown skinned,
large muscular build, nearly natty, wise, gentle man
I fell in love with him.
He is my love

Twilight night shade of skin, broad shoulders, smooth cut
hair, rough man's man, passionate beautiful spirited man
I fell in love with him
He is my foundation, my support, the man that cherished my
soul
I felt his warm cares.

I seized his nourishment.
I tasted his love with the core of my being.
I am safe.
And time held too much when I married him.

Tall, twilight night deep chocolate brown shade of skin, large hands, nearly natty, strong, muscular build, broad shoulders, rough man's man, powerful, passionate, wise, provider, gentleman, beautiful spirited man

They are my loves.

Aunt Rose wrote a letter to me telling me about the goings-on in New Orleans. She told me how the politics were screwed up as usual and that she had moved back to New Orleans from Michigan and bought a house in our old neighborhood. Aunt Rose took me as her own the day my parents died – together. It wasn't until I turned nineteen that she went to Michigan to care for Jacques, her own son. Or, rather he kidnapped her because he wasn't leaving his mama. He brought her to school with him.

My mama's sister was a caregiver, a nurturer to all the children in the family no matter how near or far. Jacques, though, seemingly had taken all of her steam. She had lost her own child and that was it for her. In her letter, she was telling me how happy she was in her new house.

In her letter, Aunt Rose told me she ran into Kolunde and his wife at the International Festival in Marconi Meadows again and they looked happy considering Kolunde's daddy had passed.

"Wait! What!!?" "Big Alyji died! ...Huh?!!!" I thought to myself. "His wife!!?" I screamed out loud. I don't know how the letter read after that sentence. I never mustered up the courage to read it to the end. I was so afraid that the letter was going to say that he had children with this woman, the children whose names I carried in my heart until they existed. And who was this woman?! Where did she come from? Why didn't I know about her?

As I dried my tears, I quickly went to the phone booth on the corner of the Campell compound where I lived and attempted to call Kolunde. In Serekunda, there were five to six houses placed on one large mass of land, a compound. All of the compounds had plaques at the entrances with the family's surname scripted in bronze. The entire family lived there together: sisters, brothers, husbands, wives, children, mothers, great mothers, fathers, great fathers - together. They ate together. They raised the children together. They worked the compound's farmland or other family businesses - together. They watched me, together, run to call Kolunde. Needless to say, the number had been changed and I was unable to reach him.

Maybe he didn't love me after all. I have waited all of my life to love him outside of my own mind. I've tried to call him from the same booth for the past year without success.

I married him. Ade Campell. I married him and became Mrs. Tiye Campell, reluctantly. He loved me. I respected him. I was accepted as part of his family. We were together.

Anticipated lovers
half remembered
Ghosts stalk sweet love's laugh
Wintry rain sweeps darkened twilight clouds
As teardrops slowly twist the past
Anticipated lovers
half forgotten

"Ade, I have to go home." I just couldn't take it any longer. "Ade, I have to go home," is what I said right after he came. I'm sorry, but I have to go. As Ade laid there breathing hard with sweat trickling from his brow, I quickly got up, covered my mouth with my hand and ran to the shower as if I was holding back vomit. What I was holding was the sound of my soul's thunderous cry shouting out "KOLUNDE!!!!"

Ade followed, "Tiye, are you alright?! Tiye, you're scaring me! Are you okay?!" "Yes, I am Ade," very softly and sympathetically, Tiye whispered. "I must go now." "Go where?" Ade was puzzled. "I am leaving to go home, Ade. Although I am grateful to have met you, I have to return to my life in New Orleans now." How long will you be there, Tiye? You are my wife," Ade shouted because in the back of his mind he knew Tiye was returning to her one true love. Ade had been aware of Tiye's heart from the beginning. She told her story with her eyes whenever he made love to her. Ade knew, but did Kolunde?

Tiye didn't even pack her things. After stepping out of the shower, she immediately wrapped two yards of material around her and slipped her feet into a pair of handmade leather flip flops that the Campells sold, along with family-symbolled handmade bedroom sets and open air roasted peanuts, on the corner down the street – on the street.

She rushed to the top dresser drawer to grab a black and brown patterned mud cloth handbag that carried money Ade had just handed her earlier in the evening and all of her important papers. She left Ade standing in the courtyard in amazement, naked and baffled. At that moment, Ade's confusion transitioned to rage. He thought to himself, "I'm gonna kill her" as he went inside for his machete.

He began throwing oak carved furniture around the bedroom as if they were made of cardboard hoping to find his underpants, or any pants. He was going to get her! "Never in a woman's life can she just up and leave her husband. Not in The Gambia! I have a very authoritative name here in The Gambia. Who does she think she is?" He didn't find the machete.

Ade ran after Tiye with her wrapper around his waist. No shoes. No shirt. No underpants. No machete, but rage nonetheless. Ade carried enough rage at that moment to sift away life with his bare hands from a 300 pound man. He ran down the city dirt road that led to the paved city street with Tiye's wrapper around his waist and fury on his face. Luckily for Tiye, she'd hopped into a bush taxi, a van type bus used for public transportation, that just so happened to be passing as she ran out to the main street.

The driver, after dropping off all of his other passengers, transported her from her safe haven with a man who genuinely loved her to the arctic and bustling scene of panhandlers, adamant tip waging workers, up-in-your-face thieves, gardenia smelling passengers, toubabs, hustling craftsmen, aggressively rude shoving passengers, handsome traditionally or European dressed African men from all countries across the continent wearing brilliantly white smiles, and the homeless at the airport in Dakar, Senegal.

Tiye was crying when she got in with the cab driver. He wondered if her husband had beaten her. He wondered if her children had gone impudent. He wondered if her husband had gone rogue and decided to take another wife because she did not bear a man-child. He wondered, and the only reason he drove that dangerous route to the neighboring country through the tumultuous dirt roads, gaping trenches, and steep hills in the pouring rain was due to sheer nosiness.

The streets of the land are filled with whistling gossip. The driver worked as a double dipper, a city transportation employee and a seeker of a new word of gossip. He was unsuccessful with the latter.

Scarlet Red

Difference? Change?

~

"You going to Ole Skool in the Park with us?" Aunt Rose was glad to see that I was home from Africa. She understood nothing about Africa. She only knew what almost all of traditionally raised Americans know or think they know. It was far. They don't like us. Oh, and "I don't wanna go there because they po' and have AIDS."

It was truly a different world, a different scent, a different color in my mind, a totally different vibe when I got off of the plane at Louis Armstrong International Airport. What a feeling! It was hard to accept that this is the place in which I was born. It was even harder to have thrown back in my face that I too was one of those African Americans who never wanted to go to Africa. But that was a long time ago.

I remember my mama telling me that "those women are animals" as she described the pain of childbirth." They pop out the baby and move around like nothing ever happened to them!" My goodness, there is so much buried in my subconscious. Anyway, with a sigh of relief from the feeling of Aunt Rose's warm embrace, I said yeah, I' m coming to the park. I was really hoping to see Kolunde. Didn't know much about his whereabouts. All I knew was the old spots we hung out in when we were in our twenties.

Leaning on the concrete lion in the park, I began tapping my feet to the music playing in the air, "a clean -up woman is a woman who takes all the love we girls leave behind." In the middle of my finger snap, all the clouds in the sky weighed heavily on my shoulders like bricks. Where is Kolunde? Who is this woman? Will I ever see him again?

These three questions played forward and backwards, backwards and forward in my head, as if someone was hitting the play button on a recorder and evilly pressing rewind to play it over and over and over again. Then they came. There they were. Tears were rolling down my face and I couldn't control them. Where is my Kolunde? I cried like no one was there. My legs became weak; I slumped to the ground. "His wife!"

Who the hell is his wife? Self-pity and pain quickly transitioned to anger. AAAAHHHHH! AAAAAHHHHH! I began screaming at the top of my lungs, they say. "It's alright, baby," Aunt Rose said as she gently caressed my forehead. "Now, I think it's time for you to tell auntie what's going on." "You know we love you, but I can't help you when I don't know what's wrong." I opened my eyes just a little wider to see where I was...in...in a hospital. WHAT. THE. HELL!

"No!" "Wait!" "Wait! Tiye!" "Baby, please come back." Consciously, I could hear Aunt Rose calling me, but my feet were moving. My heart was racing. I couldn't stop running until it was black. I couldn't see nothing! I only heard a loud noise then I was flat on my back with a blood covered face.

"I'm sorry, Mrs. Mercadel, we're going to have to keep Tiye in our facility for closer observation after the second anxiety attack. The incident this evening was a bit nasty. She has broken her nose and torn veins when snatching out the IV. Her heart rate is slightly abnormal at this time. We are doing everything we can to assist her in regaining consciousness. But we believe she will be alright." "Can I see her?" Aunt Rose asked. "She's in ICU at this time because of her heart condition so there's a limitation on visitors. But I'll come out to get you in just a few minutes."

"What is this chile doing to herself! I told her all her life that stress kill," Aunt Rose mumbled to herself while hanging and shaking her head with the agony and anguish she carried for Tiye. "What is the problem, my baby?"

Ivory and Scarlet

Change

~

As quiet somber quickly twisted, turning into a neighborhood catastrophe, especially because the going home celebration had taken so long to plan, I sat at my father's casket. Sage stood behind me and both our heads were hung in sorrow. Alyji Timpton has become an ancestor. My mind was silenced in the midst of the violent shouting by the men who stood as staples of the corner store for years. They were celebrating. Skipping and hopping and stooping and jumping with the rest of the congregation as a brass band played in the church after the wake services. It was no certain surprise that they had come to see my father off. It was also no certain surprise that they were drunk.

We, Sage and I, were just there quietly reflecting on a life of heartbreak. I guess it had taken a little longer for Tamalah to kill my daddy. It had taken just a little bit longer for him to catch up with the love of his life, my mama. He stopped eating. Vodka and tonic became his best friends, just like hip hop was mine. The memories he held of my visits to the south to feed him had become his lifeline, just like Tiye was mine. Memories.

Binta hugged my neck from behind while I sat in the chair at the casket right at that moment of overwhelmingly flooding memories. She seems to always know when I need a hug.

She seems to also know that my heart is divided. God, I love this woman. Binta is always here for me. She nurtures almost every fiber of my being. Mrs. Timpton is the best thing in my life. She holds me down; she is truly a support to my backbone.

Seems as though everybody who ever lived in the Ninth Ward for the last forty years was at my father's house later. After the funeral, my daddy's neighbor's and Binta, my wife, welcomed everyone to a potluck dinner. It had been a long time since seeing everyone, so I was grateful. There were even a few members of the Mercadel family here, including Auntie Rose.

I wondered if she had ever been able to get in touch with Tiye. I wondered if she was ok. I didn't EVER want to ask Auntie Rose these questions though. She always made it painfully clear that Tiye and I made the biggest mistake of our lives. I didn't want to have that conversation with her in Binta's presence. Binta is already not convinced that Tiye is only my childhood friend after the stories I've told her. She says my stories carry a vibration that says otherwise. And Rose Mercadel is not the most poised elder. However, she is sweet as pie.

Binta grew up in Brooklyn, but was born in Ndar, Senegal where her parents moved from. Her mother and father were traditionally initiated priests who had battled the French domination of their hometown's collective mindset. We met at a bembe held at her parents' house in Brooklyn. I would often find a place in Brooklyn to appease my soul. Baba Akojome, Binta's baba, was a strong and powerful wisdom-filled man. He was one of the first people I met outside of the drum troupe.

Baba and Binta began showing me around Brooklyn as if I were part of the family. They took me in. Mama Fatou always prepared the best Fish Yassa or Chebu Jen that was on the table as soon as we walked back in the door. She knew those were my favorite dishes and I can eat them every day. I shared my stories with them, and they shared their home with me. I was fully moved-in after six months of being in Brooklyn. They are good people. Binta is a good woman. I married her in my eleventh month as a Brooklynite. We have, since, been in delightful cordialness.

At the repass, Auntie Rose walked over to greet Sage first. Sage was knocking on his head like a friendly neighbor knocked on a front door to deliver greetings and invite you to their cookout. No one was alarmed because this was a habit for Sage. She bear-hugged him and kissed him. I watched. She didn't really know Sage. All she knew of him was we were cousins and "he looks so sad all the time." That's what she say to me every time I see her. "He looks so sad all the time, my baby."

When she finally let him go, she walked over to me. I watched her and she floated in slow motion from my view with her own soundtrack playing in my head. All I heard was a song from the movie, Claudine. "I have my reasons and they wonder why. So there's a few times sometimes I cry." I guess that song represented all that she offered to me and Tiye throughout our growing years. She taught strength and courage without parting her lips. She also always taught us to own our own truth. Her voice, when she spoke to me, often sounded like Gladys Knight singing that song. It's funny how I remember that movie considering "Claudine" came out the year I was born.

I wondered if Tiye is ok. I wondered if she would hold on when or if I ever introduced her to Binta. I wondered if I would be able to hold on to my Bonita Applebum, and Binta too. Tiye is like a hip hop song. She gotta put me on.

"Hey, Auntie Rose," I said under my breath as she seemed to want to squeeze me to where my father is now. Auntie Rose said, "Hey, my baby. I'm so sorry for your loss, chile. Hold on. I miss you, ya know. You ain't been 'round to see me since Tiye moved to Africa. I don't understand that and thangs, but I do understand you know you got people that love you, darling. You got to come around." "Ok, Auntie Rose," I said. "Good to see you too." I was looking around the house for Binta while Auntie Rose was squeezing the life outta me.

Back at the hospital with Tiye, Auntie Rose said, "Tiye, baby? It's your Aunt Rose. How you feeling, my baby? The doctors say I can take you home in the morning." Tiye answered, "I'm here, Aunt Rose. I'm ok. What the doctors say?" "They say you had a series of anxiety attacks, but you'll be fine. But, baaaabay, you have to let go the stress. What's going on? I told you Auntie can't help you if she don't know what's wrong." Aunt Rose walked across the hospital room to the window to stare out. "…and they say you're going to have a baby."

Yeah, I knew about the baby. I just was wishing somehow it could turn into just a bad dream. I did love Ade. But I do not love him like I love my Kolunde. I was to only bear Kolunde's seeds. Perhaps, I can still wish this away. So I ignored Aunt Rose's last statement.

My Aunt Rose takes care of me. She always has. I love her dearly. Since my mama passed away, Aunt Rose has loved me and cared for me immensely. She's getting older now. It's my turn to show her the same love and support she has shown me since I was a child. "Yes, I'm ready to go home, Aunt Rose. I'm staying here in New Orleans and I'm going to take care of you."

"Chile, please! Take care of me. You the one in the hospital!"

Laughter is good for the soul.

Confusion tells me that I don't want to be in holy matrimony with him
Because loneliness haunts my soul and unfaithfulness is at my spiritual rim
Suffocated love tells me that I am dying
I am no longer the same blossoming woman
I am walking dead
I cannot breathe
I am not nourished
I cannot be
I have made the biggest mistake and feel it in my every limb
For the next mistake after marriage was the baby I am carrying was conceived with him
What a blessing to have possessed the ability to bring forth life!
What pain to have acquired a numbed heart
What am I to do about the curse of the unhappy pot-bellied wife?
What detriment to have a home falling apart
As I take a step and render forth my hand

As I cover my mouth with hopes of savored breath
I am unable to stand the back woods and wastelands of the
field that I am standing Alone
Alone, with a fertilized egg in my womb
I am dying
Rubbing my stomach filled with mixed emotions
Realizing the thomp I just felt was my unborn
Sworn to nurture by nature, I love this child
Secretly

Chartreuse

Tiye

~

Each weekday morning in Treme, there was a group of tender-aged elementary school children gathering at a fish market to prepare for a trek across train tracks and a busy avenue to get to school. I was the youngest. Every day, I walked with the "big children" to school. They weren't really "big children" at all. But they were fifth and sixth graders and I was a kindergartener. They were big children to me.

We walked, and they talked and ran and played over cracked glass and used needles. They talked about toys they wanted. They talked about being hungry. They talked about cars and sports dreams, as most of them were boys. They laughed and talked and we walked to school every day for almost two years – together. They sometimes carried me on their backs because I was clumsy.

Those walks were the start of my school days. Those walks were my educational journeys. Those walks taught me that there was something wrong because we didn't live life like the children I saw on television. We didn't even look like them. Those walks reminded me that we were all from either single-family homes or challenged family homes whose members were taking the best paths available for survival. Those walks taught me that, even though we were together as a group, we faced danger each morning we stepped outside to walk from the housing experiment.

Every morning, they walked alone from the courts they lived in and waited for me to cross the street from my mama's project apartment, her first apartment when moving from my grandparents' house across the canal where most of the rest of my family lived, to get to the fish market. Those walks taught me that I was protected by my makeshift big brothers because they stood up for me when their big friends called me "blackie" or "burnt fotty girl." They tripped me when they saw me spinning or ticking and tilting my chin to the sky. Those walks taught me more how to stand up for myself, even against the "big children," and to be stern. Those walks taught me that there had to be something beyond the fishbowl where we lived.

Everyone seemed happy. My days were filled with laughter and learning. I became a sponge, directed by lessons that were both good and bad. I had become the student known for being sent to the office for defense fighting. I had not been fighting over the usual reasons that caused school fights. For that reason, I would be sent to the office to relax.

For example, other students would sometimes test my teacher-given authority to watch the class while they stepped out the room. I can recall a time when one boy called me a bitch for writing his name on the board. He proceeded to walk to the board to write the word bitch for the rest of our classmates to see. He spelled it wrong and I made sure he knew. The unfortunate moment, for me, proved to be when a teacher walking pass who heard me yelling in his face, "No, you spell bitch B-I-T-C-H, witcho 61tooped ass!"

He swung and missed. I swung and connected and stomped him and threw a chair, connecting again. The principal called my mama that time. Yes, everyone seemed happy. Underneath, everyone was angry and acting out on that anger, especially the children.

I was a studious oxymoron. I became crowned queen of my elementary school when I was in first grade. I enjoyed my teachers and they enjoyed and loved me. They really genuinely loved me. My teachers all had a relationship with my mother. They had the type of relationships shared by old friends who held phone conversations that were full of jokes and laughter. My neighbors in Treme all shared similar relationships. My teachers were my neighbors. They were my community. My community looked like me.

From those daily walks to school, I learned more about my neighborhood from my makeshift brothers and my teachers – my community. I learned about the challenges my community faced from afterschool programs that taught me dope is death. I learned, all by ear hustling without speaking a word from afterschool programs, my teachers, my family, and even community members I didn't necessarily know, that my community faced hard times with housing, with injustices, with finances; we faced challenges for *being*. I learned this very real lesson starting when I was a first grader.

On my way to second grade, I had already been placed in "gifted" classes. My new teacher didn't really look like me though. She carried a last name that can be traced to West Africa, or a last name that can be traced to the Philippines for sure. Besides my mama and daddy, my grandfather, and auntie, she was my best friend. She became one of my mama's closest friends. I'd always had a thing for big people.

It was by the second grade, too, that I had been diagnosed with a brain tumor the size of a golf ball. I was born with it. My mother received this news after she had gone through "hell and high water," as my grandmaw would say. I listened to the accounts told by my mama, my daddy, my grandpaw, my auntie, my teachers, my neighbors, my community about receiving medical assistance. I learned, then, that my community faced challenges with the medical industry too.

They were all there – my mama, my daddy, my auntie, and my Filipino teacher, and my neighbors were on standby waiting to appear at the hospital as alternates. They were all there at the hospital with me for surgery. They were all there as gatekeepers to monitor a system that they did not trust.

The last thing I remember before falling asleep from anesthesia was my auntie moving from a demeanor that was as calm as a river to raging waters of a wide sea. A staff person left me on a gurney in the busy hallway of the most popular and frequented hospital by all of New Orleans, surrounding cities, and near-by states.

Charity Hospital was a hospital known for its third floor being reserved for "crazy" people and the rest of the floors being roamed by patched up gunshot victims and overdose patients. It was also a teaching hospital that was revered for producing doctors nationwide. My auntie fought for me.

I remember the police were there – not only hospital security but the city's police, NOPD. Aunt Rose was almost arrested. She fought for my mama and my daddy who was recovering from momentary sorrow and becoming paralyzed because they had been told their little girl may not survive. And if so, would function at less than average with no chance of fully developing mental capacity. Aunt Rose fought for my family and other people at the hospital because of the way they were being disrespected and spoken to by the doctors serving a community that didn't look like them. She got results. My teacher got my hand as I was being rolled out of the hallway. I fell asleep.

I returned to the same elementary school after a while. Things were different. We no longer lived in the housing experiment, but in apartments about five or six city blocks away, apartments the community called scattered sites. I was unable to use the right side of my body. I had to learn motor skills again. But I was able to walk without falling, without being clumsy. I had to wear eyeglasses. I had no hair in the back, only ugly scars and stitches. Imagine that existence for a second grader.

But I had a bedroom with two windows. I looked out of one of those windows all the time to see the "Dope is Death" banner that hung from the interstate across the street. I looked out of that window all the time to see the brass bands and Mardi Gras Indians pass by.

I climbed out of that window often to run down the street to see the break dancers practice. I met a lot of people, big people, when we moved to our new apartment. Well, no. I didn't really meet them. I listened to them as they talked and organized against community challenges I had learned of when I was in the housing project.

I'd seen the comradery, the relationships, the building up and down my street. I learned the community members on Gov. Nicholls St. were good gatekeepers for each other. I didn't know their names mostly and they didn't know mine – I don't think. However, they knew I lived on that street and watched over me. I watched them as I grew. They watched me as I grew. They watched me walk down the street to summer camp at the church. They watched me walk down the street to get my little brother from the community center after school. I saw groups of people organizing on my walks. And every time we made it home, I would overhear my mama and her sister talking about what was happening in our community.

My mama's sister, Aunt Rose – the one who would fight a million men standing over me. My mama's big sister – the one who loved me and comforted me and taught me to play Spades when I was a child. My Aunt Rose – the one who died nine months after I came home from Serekunda, the one who has now joined her son, Jacques. My Aunt Rose, and my mama, and my daddy, and my cousin, and my Kolunde are all gone away from me. Oh, what is life!

Gold

Remembering Jacques

~

Jacques and Aunt Rose moved to Grand Rapids, Michigan after her sister was killed in a car accident. Jacques had been accepted into an art institute. He vowed, even as a young boy, to never leave his mama behind like his daddy did. He never even knew his daddy. But he knew from ear hustling that he was alive somewhere and made the excuse of "not ready to be a father" when his mama told him she was pregnant. Jacques packed up his and his mama's things and traveled north for school.

As a teenager, he was a visual artist and film director. Jacques, though, was well-known in The City of New Orleans for his immaculate murals tagged "visceral" on the sides of buildings that stood as long as the city itself. He painted realistic-looking scenes of traditionally dressed Native and African Americans attempting to live in harmony with hegemony. He painted melancholy scenes of black crying mothers with half-clothed infants and gun-toting teen boys. He painted murals of young curvaceous black girls in black and white that resembled the photographs birthed by Gordon Parks in the 1940s and 50s, images that undeniably told a story of blaxploitation. But, through all of his art, Jacques' paintings always held a gold streak leading to brilliance despite the political and socially shook jar we lived in in New Orleans. He painted murals that depicted the telltale feelings and adaptions of a people handed down as a survival roadmap by generations exposing the people's truth, lessons learned from living.

Aunt Rose eyes sparked when she spoke of her son. He was her pride and joy. He was her reward for surviving as a struggling single mother. Although we were the same age, Jacques was my big brother growing up in Treme. I never saw him much though. He was always out seeking his next brick and mortar lick. But I smelled him every night. He would always stick his head in my bedroom door to make sure I was there and fast asleep before he went home, two apartment doors down. My mama made a key for him because Jacques often said he was the man of two households, ours and his mama's. I never went to sleep until I smelled sandalwood, the oil he wore faithfully.

He was off to school to follow his passions and he carried with him his most cherished – his mother. No one knew he was sick. He was always tall and slim. No one paid attention to him getting too thin. He didn't know he was sick. He knew he didn't have an appetite anymore, but he made sure to stay hydrated. Doctors in Grand Rapids told Aunt Rose he was sick after she found him doubled over, head-first, in the bathtub in their new apartment and had him rushed to the hospital. Doctors told my auntie his kidneys had failed and he had liver cancer.

Jacques had to have known something was wrong. He had to have been in pain. But it is a known visceral fact that black men do not go to western doctors unless there is no other option. It was too late. After our sophomore year, mine at Starks U. in New Orleans and his at The Institute for Cultural Arts in Michigan, it was too late. Jacques was sent home bed ridden and mentally defeated, thinking it a curse that his life hadn't yet ended – until Kolunde visited him. After that visit, Aunt Rose said Jacques smiled at her every day until his last day.

She sees with her heart
Looking through each beat of that muscle
As she scrambles along in the city
Snapping her fingers to a sultry blues tune in her head
She sees with her heart
Dead are the nerves that run from her mind that would
otherwise
Signal her heart to listen
To reason
Hear the rhythm of time bursting out jazz rifts
Swing, bee bop, to remind her of life experience under her
feet
But she steps to each beat blindly
Led by her heart
Purposely
Refusing to the weeds sprouting from the garden inside her
heart,
Where she lives
She just wants to tip and tap to the music playing in her head
And beat the muddy pottage under her feet
And step, go, run from reality
Wanting to barter with her lifetime, weary of living blind

But her heart sees more
Her heart sees more than jivers, connivers, fast-talking liars
The ones who forget their own lies and think that they're true
The ones who smile at you and with a slow pivot, mental
bullets they shoot
They kill.
They the ones that kill the spirit
Boxing up that which is free
But her heart sees more
Her heart sees more than well- rehearsed conscious like
people
Lying through their teeth
She sees more than political snakes
Wiping out the masses to cover their own asses
She sees more than goblins dressed in religious garb
executing folk in the name of the lord
So, she stays in the garden, in her heart
Humming to the tunes in her head
Making strange rhythms with her feet
Trying to numb the feelings from her flesh
Living in the city
Only existing to outsiders, crazily
Blindly and brokenheartedly
But she's watching
Time

"Sage is gone," Binta yelled from the porch. "His clothes are gone!" Since Big Alyji's funeral, Sage had been funny-acting. He has been real, real distant-like. I did my best to try to crack that ironclad shell he built around himself. All he would say is, "Kolunde, go 'head, man." He shooed me with a three-finger motion every time.

Vodka Tonic and heroin had become Sage's comfort. I watched him start to run the streets just like I did Tamalah. I had to rely on the corner store drunk men to tell me that he was alive and still around before he disappeared from Big Alyji's house, the house we all shared – me, Binta, and Sage. After I heard Binta shouting, I went to the corner store. The drunk men were quiet when they saw me walk up and just looked at me and rustled the brown paper bags that wrapped their drink of the day.

"What's up?" I asked the four men leaning on the wall of Bar Gold's Liquor Store and stood over the one that sat on a red milk crate that barely held him because of missing crossed plastic grids. "Where my cousin?" They was a choir then, rippling a variant of mumbling octaves until meeting vocals in unison, "We don't know, man." The one who sat on the milk crate then said, "I ain't see that dude."

Who they think they talking to? Lying to? I know these drunk fools. They know I know them – and well. They know that I know when they stammer like this, they know something. Ima have to go the alternate route. I snatched my Rogue out the holster. "Where my cousin?" Them staggering drunk fools couldn't run, so they surrendered.

"Man, look. Let me tell you," one of them said while the other ones stuttered, "I...I... III...think last night we saw him. Yeah, we saw him last night." "Doing what?" I asked. One drunk said, "He was walking. He had a bag and a beer. Then them dudes..." "What dudes?" I demanded. He said he didn't know them. I asked him to describe what he saw. I quickly caught myself in mid-sentence: these cats can't describe shit – drunk bastards.

"I don't know none that. All I know is they snatched him in the car, and we been trying to see if they gon come back and snatch somebody else. Man, it could be one of us." Another drunkard said, "Look, I don't know if he got in the car 'cause he wanted to or they put his ass in there! But we ain't ask no questions."

So I searched and searched and asked questions and filed a police report and searched some more. I went to the police station to file another report and see if I can help the search party. Binta searched. My neighbors searched. We never saw Sage again. The city has a way of swallowing people.

Faded Black

Tiye and Kolunde

~

"The Calinda is the dance I danced in my dream. It is the dance of the ancestors when they celebrated self and invited one another into relationships. I was always adorned with soft, flowing white linen that dragged behind as I stepped forward with a tall beautiful head wrap that shimmered. The air released a romantic scent that hypnotized us as we inhaled and you took my hand, in my dream. We held hands and twirled around on sacred ground as we both inhaled the hypnotic aroma. The sweetest scent nestled the air arousing our wilds as we moved from holding hands to a full embrace. I saw Oshun as she moved her mirror toward me to shine my reflection within view. She then gave me a bouquet to remind me that I am just as charming. We swayed without a smile. I fell in love with you, in my dream. As we swayed, standing on clouds and listening to the African sounds of Alpha Blondy delicately roving through the atmosphere, we smiled. We walked, together, on the edges of paradise, hand in hand, without a word uttered but a soothing vibe that told a million stories. With your eyes, you told me that I am your wife, as you rubbed your hand along the nape of my neck. And I, quivering inside as I slightly rolled my neck leaning toward what felt so damn good. My hair became exposed and it began to cover my face, but you brushed it away and stared. Still without a word, you moved your hand though my natural tresses with one hand and gently grasped my hips with the other. I slowly moved to the chimes of the melody playing. There we stood on the edge of paradise, wanting."

~

He makes love to me
With no physical touch
But in such a way my core covets
He takes me soaring high
I shudder as his voice launches vibrations down my spine
I arch my back to his every oral caress
I rest my thighs and wrap my arms around his cleverness
I open my heart
I open my essence
Open to his visions as he receives mine
Open to his dreams as we entwine
our minds, our spirits, our souls embrace
He makes love to me
He seems to be the sun
And like the glimmering stars, if that is so,
I will stand as the ripened moon
With him
Holistically, in perfect harmonized partnership
If he is the sun
I would be on the other side of his kingship
Masculine force
Extra ordinary light
If he is the sun by day
I'll hold the night
Immensely sparked
Dazzlingly soft
His rays would be my tools to transform the dark
Bold, but soft
Creamy and mellow
It will be my calm to allow him to brilliantly heat tomorrow
If he is the sun
Honey soaked moon

Passing sweet at dawn
To have him remember mindfulness of his macheted-heat
Nurture riddled moon
Waiting at dusk
To wrap coolness around him each time we meet
If he is the sun

"Time to get funky, new radical hip as I get to the point. Rock this funky joint." PRT was up! And the rain was pouring, drenching me and Kolunde like a hose pipe. But we was out there! Wet shive! We were dancing and singing and laughing. It was one of the best days of my life. This was the best gift for my pre-graduation celebration. It was graduation time for everyone one month before. Starks U's graduation ceremony was always late during Spring, early in the Summer.

We became the concert for the onlookers underneath the shelter. We became entertainers to the entertainment – Poor Righteous Teachers. We became closer to each other that day when we didn't even know that could be possible. Joy in its rawest form. We became more. We became inseparable by the end of the concert, seemingly. This concert and my graduation led to the last times I would be seeing Kolunde.

It's a beautiful day, I thought to myself as I sat outside at the front door of Aunt Rose's house in the neighborhood that was most familiar to me - a house that was now my own willed by my mama's big sister.

At that moment, my soul was soothed; my spirit was calm. All of my childhood memories were playing in my head like Mantronix's Needle to the Groove on a Memorex cassette tape. Spring mornings were always beautiful.

I thought about the break dancers down the street who spun on their heads and shoulders. I thought about the up-in-yo-face demands made by my mama's friends when their landlords came to collect rent. I thought about hanging around the big people as they organized against the oppressions hurled against them. I thought about how every school building in this neighborhood wore a piece of Jacques. I thought about my Kolunde, and how I wished he could have been with me as I walked down Gov. Nicholls St. to get my lil brother from summer camp. I thought about how I wished I could have shared, in more than a word, the blissful feelings that overwhelmed me when I looked out of my window at the "Dope is Death" banner under the Claiborne Bridge. I thought about Kolunde's family, cross the canal, and how he probably tucked away his sorrow and grief by now. I thought...I need to see Kolunde.

I went inside to dial the only phone number I had carried for him for the past two years. I carried that number with me like I carried the feeling of his rough but gentle touch in my repetitive dreams. I carried that one piece of torn off tarnished paper like the heart that carried scars and admiration and genuine love that had become tarnished and torn off. That heart belonged to me in this moment.

How do I see Kolunde? Does he even know I have returned? I wonder if he heard about Aunt Rose. I didn't tell many. I just prayed and danced, and laughed and prayed, and cried and cremated her, like she asked. I wondered.

He answered. Kolunde answered the phone! I almost hung up. I couldn't gather words to greet him because I didn't know how. Should I greet him over the phone like an old friend I am trying to reconnect with? Should I greet him with our favorite Pharcyde line, "I guess everybody need somebody to love. You can't keep love lonely." Should I immediately apologize for making Aunt Rose swear she would never give him a number to call me in Serekunda? I wasn't ready to face Ade and all the questions and accusations that would have come from that call. I wasn't ready to face the rest of the family's stares and smirks when his grandmaw, the one who answered the phone on the compound, yelled across the courtyard, "It's Kolunde for Tiye!" It was her usual shouting call to whoever should then rush over to the phone booth that sat on the compound like lawn furniture.

Kolunde said hello and I eventually said hi. Then, we both were silent. In the time it took for me to tap out the beat to the intro for I'm Still Number One by Boogie Down Productions on my kitchen table, Kolunde began to speak. Although he didn't directly speak to me, he began to rap – "Let us begin. What, where, why or when…" Hip hop did that for us. It always seems to know just what to say. Music had a way of helping us rest our nerves.

I'm sorry, Kolunde. I'm sorry to hear about Big Alyji. Kolunde sighed. "Tiye?" "That's what you called me to say?"

"Thank you for your condolences." Silence fell upon our receivers once more. It was the kind of silence that deafened. I then said, my Aunt Rose said the services were beautiful.

"How you just left?!" Kolunde belted out after an extremely awkward silence. "You didn't even say leaving was on your list of plans when we were together for your graduation!" "You told me you were taking a teaching gig at Tubman School in Treme!" Kolunde's words flew out with a hint of anger and I couldn't get a word in. "You said we would start an Arts program there!" "Then, poof!" "Nobody heard from you again!" "What's up?"

Kolunde, I'm sorry. "Yeah, that's sorry," he sarcastically said. "What's up? Where are you?" I'm at Aunt Rose's house in Treme. I've been back almost a year now. "A year!" This time I heard dead silence. My Kolunde. Was he really mad at me? Like – for real? After graduation, I just couldn't bring myself to have that conversation with him. How was I going to say to my best friend on the planet that I ain't gon see you again 'cause I'm moving to Africa and not coming back? How was I going to say to him that I've loved you like forever and we can never be to each other what I truly want because we have been "friend-zoned" by his choice? I wanted to tell him so many times that I never just wanted to be his friend. I wanted to be his forever wife! How can I say that? My Kolunde. My Kolunde had hung up on me and I was left with dead silence.

When I called back and he answered, we didn't say hello. He picked up the phone and I screamed out to him, I love you! Please come over here. I want to talk to you. I want to see you. I want to hold your hand and laugh just like we did at that concert.

Kolunde held the phone.

He thought about all the fun they had that day. He thought about Tiye's smile and how her curled locs draped over her face. He thought about how she looked like she was always floating in air when she walked in all of her flowing dresses. He thought about Mama Enike' and how much Tiye looked like his mama. He thought about love. Then, he thought about Binta.

"Yeah, tell Auntie Rose to cook me some cabbage." "What's the address? I knew she moved back after Jaques transitioned, but I never asked her where. Sometimes I never asked her nothing because I never could breathe when she squeezed me." Kolunde, I whispered as I tried to keep the lump in my throat from moving to my chest.

I have to tell you something about Aunt Rose. "Yeah, what?" We'll talk when you get here. We have so much to talk about. If you come by this evening, I'll have your cabbage ready. The address is 2331 Delille Street. "Yeah, Ty. We have a whole lot to talk about. I be there at 7:00. Imma bring ginger beer and some fresh gardenias for you." Kolunde always knew my favorites.

And Tiye was off! She went back outside to fold and bring the chair she was sitting in back inside. She grabbed her purse, slipped on some flip-flops and jetted out of the door she just came in – off to make groceries. She bought three heads of cabbage and smoked turkey necks. She bought jasmine rice because she didn't have enough at home to pack plates after dinner for Kolunde to bring back home for him and Sage. She bought almond milk, cornmeal, baking soda, and eggs. She already had butter, flour, and honey at home. She remembered how much Kolunde loved her corn bread.

On her way to the car, she stopped by the "incense man" and bought Frankincense oil and Sandalwood incense. This was her small offering to Kolunde. She thought to herself, the words I have to share and this dinner would be offering big, beaucoup big, enough. She also thought how Kolunde loved little gifts from her that held soft intimacy, tokens of reminders of when her life was his and his life was hers. Tiye returned home and started to cook. She blasted music loud enough for all the neighbors to hear and lit an incense. The whole street jammed to Common's "Go." She was on *go*! Tiye was *running back to her fantasy.*

Kolunde knocked on the door one nano-second after Tiye had gotten out of the shower and gotten dressed. He didn't call to say he was on his way. He just showed up and on time just like Tiye always remembered about him.

She opened the door. Kolunde was standing there bright as the sun that shined on New Orleans. He was holding a bag in one hand and a large basket of gorgeous gardenias and wore a smile that escaped all the worry Tiye held about his angered toned the last she spoke to him. He wore a smile that said more than the nonchalant "hey" greeting spoken from his lips.

Tiye was melting. She had become, in a moment, the same college freshmen standing at the elevator at Starks U. She had also become aware that she and Kolunde were standing at the wide-opened front door letting the air out the house, so she motioned for her love to come in.

"It smells good in here!" Kolunde sang as he put the basket of flowers on the coffee table. "Where Auntie Rose?" In that moment, Tiye was jerked back from her gooey love state of mind to inwardly screaming terror. How do I tell this man this? I can't tell him this now! Tiye thought to herself. Oh, we'll talk later, Kolunde, was all Tiye could manage to say.

"That was some good eating there, Tiye!" Kolunde was pleased with the food and the company. He still wondered about Auntie Rose because there was never a time he could remember that she wasn't around and squeezing life from him. He walked over to the sofa and sat. He started to gaze at Tiye. The kind of gaze that spoke a thousand words, but his gaze was one that people had when they were in deep thought and staring at nothing. In Kolunde's eyes, Tiye saw sadness and fear. She saw indecisiveness and grief. Ultimately, she saw her friend - a sensitive, yet sweet-rough man's man. She saw that she needed to somehow comfort her friend. She sat next to him on the sofa.

Kolunde immediately hugged her neck and placed his forehead on hers. He said, "let's talk." Tiye began to feel the same emotions she saw in Kolunde's eyes. She felt sadness and fear, indecisiveness and grief; but, because of Kolunde's safety net type hug around her shoulders, she felt a sighing comfort. She responded to Kolunde, "Yeah, let's talk." Kolunde, Aunt Rose transitioned a few months ago. She left me and my brother this house. My brother moved to Oakland, though, after he graduated from Starks U. He said he isn't coming back to this city and that I should transfer everything over in my name only.

Aunt Rose loved you. I thought I should say that to you. But she made me promise her that I wasn't going to have wake and funeral services for her. She wanted a quiet send off. She's here though – over there. She will always live in this house. With a real tear down his chiseled cheek, Kolunde turned to see where Tiye kept Aunt Rose's ashes.

"May she rest in perfect peace." Kolunde said as his one tear snowballed to multitude. With a deep breath, he turned to Tiye once again placing his forehead on hers. "Look, Tiye. This conversation may be blow for blow. Are we ready?" Yes, Kolunde. It has been quite a while since we have had very clear, heart-to-heart conversations. Remember when we used to sit in the park throwing dirt rocks in the water. I miss us. "Yeah, Ty. I miss us too."

"Sage is gone." Gone where?! Tiye quickly scooted to the edge of her seat on the sofa breaking the safety net that comforted her. Are you saying Sage is dead?! "No, bae. Well, I don't know if he's dead." Tiye became even more baffled. Whatcha saying, Kolunde? What you mean you don't know if he's dead? "I mean, I never got word from anybody, not even the police, telling me that they found him." "Sage just walked out the door one morning with that same busted up bag he always had from his daddy and I haven't seen him since." Oh so, you mean he moved away? "That's what I want to believe, but the old men at the corner store said they saw men pull him in an unknown car that same night and sped off. It's been months now. No Sage."

Tiye scooted back on the sofa into Kolunde's arms. I sure didn't want to hear that, Kolunde, just like I'm sure you didn't want to hear the news about Aunt Rose. Let me fix you a drink. That was heavy. "Ok, I'll take a drink 'cause, Tiye, this conversation is not over." Tiye sighed and slowly walked over to the living room bar stand. What else is it, Kolunde, she asked when she returned to her seat and her true love's arms. "I went last. It's your turn. What was ya doing in Africa? And, why didn't you tell me?" Don Julio choked Tiye, then.

When I got home after the graduation, I saw I had a missed called from one of my professors. Her message said she knew of a teach abroad assignment in The Gambia and she knew how much I wanted to go to West Arica. She said that if I decided to go, she would have the African Studies Department fund travel, lodging, and expenses for a year.

I wanted to tell you, Kolunde, but then I thought about how you always told me to follow where my skills and heart lead. I remembered how I would feel every time I thought about us, bitter-sweet and sometimes downright horrible. I never wanted to just be your friend, Kolunde. I never wanted to wreck the movement in your career either. I thought I would only be in the way of your concert tours. I was wrong. Yes, I know before you even tell me so. But I wanted you to also follow your skills and your heart. I didn't think I was in your heart like you were in mine, so I left.

Kolunde just sat there with the same silence he created on the morning phone call. He eventually whispered, "So how was teaching in The Gambia?" Wait, that's not all, Kolunde. Tiye knew Kolunde well. She knew that he would change the subject of conversation to avoid the hard point of what was being said, just like she would often do. I love you, Kolunde. I've always loved you. It scared me and that's why I left.

I met a man there. "Oh, yeah," Kolunde sat up and said. Yeah. "Word" Tiye sipped faster on the Don Julio that just about choked her to darkness. I married him. "Oh, yeah. So, where he at?" He's in The Gambia. I got a letter from Aunt Rose one day and she was telling me how much fun she had at the summer hip hop concert that year. I think she really wanted me to know that she actually went. I was so happy to hear she actually went! But also, in her letter, she told me you had a wife. Do you have a wife, Kolunde? Tiye already knew this to be fact because Aunt Rose wouldn't tell anything else.

Kolunde sat back and relaxed his back on the sofa, this time without his arm wrapped around Tiye. They both sat in the same way on the sofa while holding their drinks that dripped from melting ice. Staring. At nothing. …until Tiye got up to fix more drinks.

As soon as Tiye sat back down, Kolunde blurted, "...so I think you were married before me." So, that means you do have a wife? "Yes, her name is Binta." Tiye's head felt, at that time, as big as the hoop earrings she wore still because they reminded her of the greatest era of her life. She began to sweat like African drummers in the height of any rhythm they played. Her anxiety peaked to heights that would call attention to any therapist. Then Kolunde hugged her. She immediately calmed down and all worry that had consumed her when she thought Kolunde was about to tell her about his children. She learned he didn't have any children.

"You left me, Tiye. I loved you!" You don't love me anymore? "Yes. I love the earth that secures your ancestor guided steps. I love the air you inhale that nourishes your lungs as you prepare to speak with a melody only I hear. I love your caring and mother-like demeanor. I love who you are, Tiye. I've always loved you." Tiye had never heard Kolunde express himself in that way before. She placed her forehead back on his and she cried, silently.

Their silence spoke boisterous designation in many languages and dialects. She finally said, "...but Kolunde, I left him. I left Ade. In The Gambia. I left him to come home to look for you. Tiye didn't want to alarm Kolunde by telling him her first week back was spent at Charity Hospital. Not just then anyway.

Kolunde turned to look in Tiye's eyes, preparing himself to tell her more about Binta. But Tiye quickly said there's more. I had an abortion. When I came home, I was carrying his baby. Kolunde began to drink his Hennessey as if he was drinking water. "Why did you have an abortion?" Kolunde asked. I had an abortion because I never wanted to birth anyone's children unless their last names were Timpton. Kolunde stood up and so did Tiye. They both put their drinks down on the coffee table coasters next to the basket of gardenias. They were in a full embrace as their eyes met after looking away from the basket bouquet. He rubbed her hair.

"Binta moved here from New York after we got married. She is good to me. She knows my heart is with you. She is still good to me. She's a strong woman. And she loves me." Never letting go of the embrace hold, Tiye looked up at Kolunde with tears on her face. She kissed him. So, I guess this is when all that time has held changes for us, Tiye said. "But I'll never stop loving you," Kolunde added. He kissed her. And this time held too much.

Emotional colors masking dissipating despair
Every human sense, in this moment, alert but unprepared for
honeysuckle scented inhales pumping soft iridescent
message hues
to the brain stem. As silent screams wail, shooting hard-
shocked visual indigo blues
but I'm with him
And I'm open
Hoping he catch the rhythms of each sporadic wave down my
back.
Wanting him to squeeze the largest curve of me and breathe
at the nape of my neck.
I'm open
Soaking up all my walls more with each nibble
Tremble at every thigh tingle as we toss and turn
Unconsciously parting my lips more with each playful bite and
caress,
wondering which other parts will he address and learn
Melting
Sparked coal
Moistened onyx skin
Rub placing and tasting buds
Out and in
Loving how our souls are being nourished and felt
Our limbs wrapped around each other like an octopus belt.
I'm open
Licking and sucking and pulling and kiss
Breathing and swelling and pinching and this...
the entry and my bliss
And his groans and my moans and my muscles and my skin
and our tussles
And our toes and his chill bumps and my sweat, on his neck

My cheek smashed against the delicate hairs on his chest
And stubble on his cheeks and his neck, sensational rest
And my breast on his tongue
Nipples erect.
And our fingers, at their tips, down our cracks react like fate.
Then, the hairs on our bodies stood straight.
I'm open
Sweet melodic baritone in my ear
Closed lids sight ocean waves under sunset while dropping
tears.
The relief. No fear.
The release. No words
but at least, no grief.
We smiled.

It was all in the open now. They had aired out years of life in a few words. They had released what had been bonding them both with thick, tight splintered ropes. They were still bonded. Bonded by what would never leave their gut. They slept.

It was then morning. Kolunde got up from bed to walk to the bathroom to refresh for the new day. He had no worries about Binta. He knew Binta was going to be pissed. He also knew Binta was going to be there. At his house. "She'll never leave," he thought to himself. "But I want Tiye to stay." Tiye got up from bed to walk him to the door. They embraced each other. Kolunde left.

Tiye sat on the floor at the coffee table sniffing her gardenias and wondering can this city be big enough for the three of us.

Author's Commentary

Black Family Synchronization Across Culture

With viewing this story through an anthropological lens, I have realized I have made many observations throughout the span of my lifetime. These observations have been written in books, been coined and theorized over several years. However, these observations have not only been a stamp for accredited academia for me. Unlike many cultural anthropologists of whom I am familiar, these observations have told the story of my existence. I am not an outside observer. I am a part, by birth, to what others have only been spectators as they work to understand and imitate their observations.

I am living a life with an overhead designed by the construction of social hierarchies and political dominance. I am also living a life partnered with people, black communities, who expose, counter, and challenge imposed dominance but "to believe [that said dominance doesn't exist,] otherwise would threaten a key assertion of American ideology; that all Americans enjoy an equal opportunity for success (Robbins, R.H., 2006, p. 247, Ch. 7). All Americans do not enjoy equal opportunities; nevertheless for success, but all Americans do not enjoy equal opportunities in humanity.

Communities in New Orleans are all too familiar with generational experiences and reactions to those experiences triggered by the suffrage from constructs to socially inform the people of what is intelligence, what is the proper language to use, who has human rights, what is reality. I grew up in a family, unlike many others, and neighborhoods that address these constructs with an answer that is not verbally spoken sometimes, but is acted out – that answer is often, "It is what I say it is." We often *make due* by living parallel to what is believed to be social normalcy for survival like our grandparents did and like their grandparents did. This way of living is normal in New Orleans.

At times in the story, Kolunde and Tiye walk readers through lived insanity or what can be viewed as insanity in other parts of the country. Readers are able to walk along with them on physical paths while going in and out of consciousness at the same time. I have observed, even that of my own self, people in New Orleans to live in this way - daily. Some professionals may label it as a coping mechanism. I would say cultural and Creative Arts in New Orleans is the surviving apparatus. It is the resiliency machine generating and spotlighting shared experience, comradery, language, healing, and education. It is a distinguished language seemingly only New Orleanians deeply share, even without knowledge that they may be doing so.

Rhythm is healing. It is rhythm, in whichever form, that gives strengthened perseverance through any struggle. In the Psychotherapy field, there is even a healing practice termed "tapping" or the Emotional Freedom Technique (EMT). In Behavior Analysis, there is what is termed "stimming" (or Self Stimulatory Behavior) associated with Autism.

Creative Arts are greatly used as imaginative and rhythmic coping skills for cognitive-emotional stamina to battle grief, anxiety, and depression. Play and music therapy are even offered from licensed professionals. However, Let Me Taste depicts how these coping skills are inherited. These skills are all produced as second nature, without one charging another hundreds of dollars to assist or studying to write a peer-reviewed article about "how they do it." In black communities, it is done as second nature inherited from past generations. Paid counseling, when needed, is also beneficial to black families. Acceptance and trust of trained therapists, though, have not been passed down through generations. So, guess what usually happens.

Abandonment or abrupt aloneness is another phenomenon that is studied and "victims," as seen by society, are prescribed destructive medication to treat outward behavioral explosions without learning a root cause for feelings that are largely believed to be unreal.

Tiye loved Kolunde. There is no doubt. Kolunde loved her. However, Tiye's love seemed to be self-destructive due to her emotional need for protectors and people with whom she could mutually share life lessons or the beauty of life as seen by her which, in her mind, because of society's constructs, were strangely eclectic. She loved Kolunde for other reasons as well, but the attacks were rooted in her fight for retention of a man who truly loved her in all her bizarre shyness and sharp-witted intelligence.

Society has told black women that they are not enough or ugly and unworthy by any meaning or applied aspect of the words. Inasmuch, some women battle to keep protection nearby or know where to pull it from if and when protection from societal constructs is needed. Tiye's father could not protect her. He did not protect her mother. Tiye's mother was her own protector and Tiye's protector as well. Aunt Rose protected everybody and was the protector of the protector in the family, Jacques, until he became of age.

Kolunde held all of the qualities and character that Tiye fantasized her protector would possess. Although she attempted to move on with her life, Tiye only wanted to live her life with Kolunde. He treated her in a way that defied society's constructs. He saw her as beautiful, smart, a healing force, soft but not fragile, deserving of all things hoped for yet independent enough to acquire those things on her own. He was her net and her propeller.

In closing, I would like to challenge you to observe and dream. Listen to those who have lived life before you. Live. Write. Dance. Draw. Laugh. Love. I challenge you to live before you die. All too often, we are consumed with other people's constructs. Be aware of the emotional and physical devastation mirrored to us as self-hate, often rooted in the effects of political dominance and social hierarchical disasters. This hate for one another often leads to violence within our communities. Live in a manner that sits outside of those mental confines to truly expand and celebrate who you are as an artist. You are an artist by design! You are a healer by design! Together, we are love by design!

Reference:

Robbins, R. H., (2006). Cultural Anthropology A Problem-Based Approach. 4th Edition. California, Thomas Wadsworth